Grasshopper MAGiC

Grasshopper MAGiC

by Lynne Jonell
illustrated by Brandon Dorman

A STEPPING STONE BOOK™
Random House 🏠 New York

To Marlene Glaus, my wonderful third-grade teacher,
with thanks and love—L.J.

For Max, our little hop-jumper—B.D.

Text copyright © 2013 by Lynne Jonell
Jacket art and interior illustrations copyright © 2013 by Brandon Dorman

Visit us on the Web!
SteppingStonesBooks.com
randomhouse.com/kids

Educators and librarians, for a variety of teaching tools,
visit us at RHTeachersLibrarians.com

Library of Congress Cataloging-in-Publication Data
Jonell, Lynne.
Grasshopper magic / by Lynne Jonell ; illustrated by Brandon Dorman. — 1st ed.
p. cm. — (Magical mix-ups ; 3)
"A Stepping Stone Book."
Summary: To prove he is brave enough to portray his ancestor in a town parade,
Abner Willow eats a bowlful of fried grasshoppers and suddenly gains the magical
ability to leap and jump.
ISBN 978-0-375-87084-2 (trade) — ISBN 978-0-375-97084-9 (lib. bdg.) —
ISBN 978-0-307-97469-3 (ebook) — ISBN 978-0-307-93123-8 (pbk.)
[1. Courage—Fiction. 2. Grasshoppers—Fiction. 3. Parades—Fiction. 4. Magic—
Fiction. 5. Brothers and sisters—Fiction.] I. Dorman, Brandon, ill. II. Title.
PZ7.J675Gr 2013
[Fic]—dc23   2011053002

Printed in the United States of America
10 9 8 7 6 5 4 3 2 1

Random House Children's Books supports the First Amendment
and celebrates the right to read.

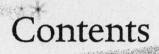

Contents

CHAPTER 1

Are You Chicken?

"No," said Abner. "I don't want to do it."

He didn't want to go downstairs and barge into his parents' party. He didn't want to dodge through a crowd of strangers to get to the dessert table. And he didn't want to load a plate with little iced cakes and try to bring them back. For one thing, he would look like a pig.

"But you're the oldest," said Celia.

Derek said, "You're the tallest, too."

Tate flipped her ponytail over her shoulder. "You're the closest to being a grown-up," she explained. "You'll blend in better than we would."

Abner pointed at their supper trays. "If you're so hungry, why don't you finish the party food you already have?"

Derek popped a tiny meatball in his mouth. "There," he said with his mouth full. "That's the last good thing. Everything else is weird."

Tate waved a hand at the food that was left. "He's right, Abner. Look. Cream cheese and peppers. Stuffed mushrooms. Watercress and pickled beets and—what *is* that green stuff?"

"Roasted Brussels sprouts," said Derek in a tone of gloom. "I asked."

Abner looked at the round green vegetables and flinched.

"But the *cakes* were good," said Tate, smiling brightly.

"Only there weren't enough of them," Derek added.

Celia snuggled up next to Abner and opened her blue eyes as wide as she could. "I like the ones with pink icing the best of all," she said. "Make sure to get lots of those."

Abner sighed. Celia was the littlest, and it was hard to say no to her. But he hated crowds of strangers. And he was shy around grown-ups. They always asked him what he wanted to be when he grew up, and he never knew how to answer.

Derek looked at him sideways. "You're not *scared*, are you?"

Abner scowled. Of course he wasn't scared.

"We'll come with you part of the way," Tate said.

"Oh, all right," said Abner.

Laughter and the clink of glasses could be

faintly heard two floors down. The four Willow children took off their shoes and tiptoed, sock-footed, down the stairs.

They stopped at the second-floor landing, which overlooked the entry hall. They could hear the party in the next room. A babble of adult voices swirled up the stairs.

Abner took a deep breath. He *wasn't* scared. But what if someone bumped into him when he was carrying the plate of little cakes? He would drop them all and probably break the plate, too.

"What are you waiting for?" asked Derek.

"Don't rush me." Abner leaned over the banister for a better look. There was no one in the hall, but the kitchen door was open. Maybe there were extra cakes in the kitchen?

Abner ran down the stairs. He saw two trays of pink and white cakes on the kitchen counter. No one stopped him or even seemed

to notice as he carried a tray up to the landing.

Tate, Derek, and Celia gave him a silent cheer and many pats on the back. They sat on the floor and each took a cake. Derek took two.

"We don't need forks or plates," Tate said.

"Our hands are pretty clean." Then she looked at Derek's and changed her mind. "Mine are, anyway."

Derek had found a way to keep crumbs from falling onto the floor. "If I tip my head back and hold the cake over my mouth, all the crumbs drop right into it," he said.

The party was getting louder. Celia stopped in the middle of her fourth cake to listen. She heard lots of words she knew, like "willow," "parade," and "town." But they were mixed in with words she didn't know at all.

"Grown-ups always talk about things I can't understand," she said through a mouthful of crumbs. "It's boring."

Derek swallowed his sixth little cake and reached for a seventh. "Grown-up parties are boring, too. They all just stand around. They don't play any games."

"No games?" Celia was shocked. "Do they at least get goodie bags?"

Abner shook his head. "No goodie bags, no games, no pony rides, no magic tricks—"

"And no *magic*," said Tate. "Not real magic. Not like the kind that happens to us."

The others nodded. Magic *had* happened to them. Since they had moved to the house on Hollowstone Hill, it had happened twice. They weren't sure it would ever happen again, but they had hopes.

"I just wish we knew how the magic worked," said Abner. "It can get a little wild sometimes."

Derek laughed. "Remember when Celia turned into a giant hamster?" He crinkled his nose and squeaked, making a hamster face.

"You should talk," Celia said. "Remember how you couldn't make the lawn mower stop? Now *that* was funny."

Abner picked at a frayed spot on his shirt. He wished he knew more about it. He felt responsible for the others, and magic had almost gotten them into a lot of trouble.

They knew a little bit. They knew it came from somewhere underground. It could get into animals and even things, like lawn mowers. And it could be used up. But they never knew when the magic would happen, or what it would do. That made Abner nervous.

"Hey, Abs!" Tate pulled at Abner's sleeve. "Listen! Someone is talking about you!"

The lady's voice from the party room was loud and piercing. Abner stood up and leaned over the banister so he could hear every word.

"Abner Willow?" came the voice. "Your family is descended from *General* Abner Willow?"

Abner shrugged and looked back at the others. "They're only talking about the guy in the painting," he said. "You know, with the sword and the horse."

They knew. Abner was named after an elderly relative who had been some kind of hero a long time ago. There was a painting of him in a museum, and a copy of it in a book somewhere. Their parents had shown it to the children. The children hadn't been terribly interested.

All at once, some people came out of the party room with Mr. and Mrs. Willow. Abner took a step back so they wouldn't see him. His heel bumped the cake tray and it made a loud clatter.

Everyone looked up.

"Why, here's Abner now," said their father. "Come down, son. I want you to meet someone."

"Oh, my, he looks *just* like the general!" said a tall lady, clapping her hands.

Abner didn't think he looked like the general

at all. His nose wasn't as big, and he didn't have a sword or a horse. But it wouldn't be polite to tell the lady she was wrong. He walked slowly down the stairs.

"Abner," said his mother, "Mrs. Gofish tells us the town is having a parade. She thinks you can help."

The tall lady smiled at Abner. "You could help a lot," she said. "You see, every year at this time, our county has a festival we call Willow Days."

Abner was surprised. "You named a festival after our family?"

Everyone laughed. Abner's ears turned red.

"Willow Days isn't named after our family," his father explained. "It's named after the big willow trees that line the river in town."

"But it *could* be named after your family," said Mrs. Gofish, "now that we know you're related to a famous general in history. Why, he was practically born in this town!"

"Sixty miles away," murmured Mr. Willow.

"Close enough," said Mrs. Gofish, waving her hand. "I am sure he rode through town on his way to battle." She gave Abner a big smile and patted his shoulder. "You are named after a very brave man."

Abner nodded politely. He knew that. But he didn't see what that had to do with a parade.

Mrs. Gofish began to explain. She talked very fast about something called a historical society. Abner didn't know what that was. She talked about something called a grand marshal. Abner didn't know what that was, either.

But he didn't want to ask her. He already had asked one question, and the grown-ups had laughed. He wasn't about to ask any more.

He stood on one leg and then the other,

feeling hot and uncomfortable. He stared at his feet and wished he were somewhere else.

Then Mrs. Gofish said, "What do you say, Abner?"

The room grew quiet. Everyone was looking at him.

Abner didn't want to say he hadn't paid attention. He didn't want to say he had no idea what she'd been talking about.

Mrs. Gofish smiled at him again. "Let me put it another way, Abner. Would you like to help your town?"

Abner was relieved. This was an easy question. "Sure," he said. "I guess."

She clapped her hands again. "Good! Then it's settled." She turned to Abner's mother and began to talk very fast in a low voice.

Abner wondered what was settled. He heard the words "costume," "sewing," "Mrs. Delgado," and "tomorrow." But then all the grown-ups started talking at once. He backed away toward the stairs. His sisters and brother were waiting for him on the landing.

"Are you really going to lead the town parade?" Celia asked. "On a horse?" She hadn't been able to understand everything, but she had understood that much.

"You're lucky," said Derek, who had understood a little more. "I wish *I* could wear a uniform and carry a sword."

"I'm glad I'm not the one who has to pretend to be the general, though," said Tate, who had understood almost everything. "I would hate to read a speech in front of the whole town."

Abner's mouth opened. He made a strangled sound.

Had he really agreed to do all that?

His knees felt funny and weak. He sat down suddenly.

Tate sat down next to him. "Don't you want to do it?"

Abner shook his head. He kept on shaking it.

"But if you didn't want to do it, then why did you say yes?" Derek asked.

Abner was embarrassed to say that he hadn't really listened. He had been too busy worrying about all the people looking at him.

Celia had been watching her big brother with her thumb in her mouth. Now she took it out. "It's hard to say no to a grown-up lady who smiles at you."

This was very true. But it didn't make Abner feel any better.

"So what are you going to do?" asked Tate.

"You'd better practice looking brave," said Derek.

"And riding a horse," said Celia.

❦❦❦

The guests had all gone, and Mr. and Mrs. Willow were cleaning up after the party. Abner and Tate sat on the porch steps while

Derek and Celia ran around in the dusk with a jar and a tennis racket. They were catching grasshoppers.

"You won't catch many now," called Tate. "It's almost dark."

"So? It's still fun," said Derek, stirring up the long grass with the edge of his racket.

"There! I whacked one! Put it in the jar with the rest of them, Celia."

"Where did it drop?" Celia's voice floated out over the lawn in the soft summer night's air. "I can't see it."

Derek moved toward the family's vegetable garden. "Just feel on the ground for it," he said.

"Or get a flashlight. Dad will let you have one. He hates grasshoppers."

Celia set her jar on the porch steps and ran into the house.

Abner screwed the lid on a little more tightly. The grasshoppers they had caught yesterday were already dead, but the new ones were still hopping a little. Mr. Willow would be happy to see the jar. He didn't want grasshoppers eating the leaves in the vegetable garden.

"I'll pay you to catch them for me," he had said. "Two cents a grasshopper, dead or alive. And preferably dead."

Grasshoppers were hard to catch. They would whir up between your feet with a clickety sound. Then they would bound off faster than you could grab them. When Abner did catch them, he hated the dry, crinkly feel of their wings and hard bodies. So he had come up with the idea of using a tennis racket to stun them.

It worked. But he still didn't enjoy it. He was happy to let Derek and Celia earn the money. He was busy wondering what he could do about the parade.

"I've never been on a horse," he told Tate. "I'm going to look stupid, dressed up like General Willow. And I *really* don't want to read a speech." He scowled. He wished more than ever that he understood how to work the magic on Hollowstone Hill. He could use some.

Tate tried to cheer him up. "But horses are nice, and you'll look great in a uniform. You're a good reader, too. What are you so worried about?"

Abner picked at a splinter on the porch steps. "What if I fall off the horse? What if I trip over my sword when I get up to read the speech? What if I stand there and nothing comes out when I try to talk?"

Tate didn't know how to help him. "You'd better get used to the idea, fast," she warned. "The parade is the day after tomorrow."

Derek came up. "You can't back out of it now," he said. He spun his tennis racket on the bottom step.

"Well, you *could*," said Tate. "But then you'd be breaking your promise."

"Plus, everyone would know you were chicken," said Derek.

"I'm *not* chicken," Abner said. "I'm just—" He stopped. *Was* he chicken?

"Maybe you're just a little bit chicken," Tate said tactfully.

Derek stuck out his elbows and flapped as if he had wings. *"Bwack buk buk buk!"*

Abner didn't appreciate the chicken noises. He socked Derek on the shoulder. Derek whacked him over the head. There was a pleasant scuffle for some minutes, ending with Abner sitting on top of Derek. "Take it back," Abner said.

Derek wheezed. "Get . . . orf . . . me!"

"Not until you take back the chicken noises." Abner was unmoving.

"Kub kub kub," gasped Derek.

All of them understood that these were chicken noises, only backward, so Abner let Derek sit up.

"Now that that's over with," said Tate, who did not approve of violence, "I have an idea. What you need is bravery practice."

CHAPTER 2

Magic Snacks

But the next morning, before they could think of anything brave for Abner to do, Mrs. Delgado drove up in her small green car.

Mrs. Delgado was a large, solid woman with a dimple in one cheek. She was very good at sewing. The historical society wanted someone to sew a general's costume for Abner, and she was the best in town.

So Mrs. Delgado brought a tape measure,

a pincushion, and a big pair of scissors. She told Mrs. Willow that there was no time to waste.

"I have to make this uniform by tomorrow," she said. She unfolded a picture of General Abner Willow and poked her finger at it. "So I must stay here and do the fittings. And you"— she pointed at Abner—"are going to stand still for me, no?"

"Er . . . ," said Abner. He had a feeling she meant "yes" when she said "no," but he wasn't sure. And because she said her words with a different accent, it took him a minute to figure out what she had said.

Mrs. Delgado laughed, and her whole body shook. "You have trouble understanding me," she said, "because I am not born in this country. But you will get used to the way I talk, no?"

"No," said Abner. "I mean, yes." He nodded

so she would know he was trying to agree with her.

Mrs. Willow smiled and cleared a space on the dining room table for Mrs. Delgado to work. "I have to go to town," she said, "but I left sandwich fixings in the refrigerator. You children can make your own lunch. Be sure to help Mrs. Delgado all you can."

"Good," said Mrs. Delgado. "They can help carry my sewing things from the car!"

Abner staggered under the weight of three bolts of fabric. Behind him, Mrs. Delgado carried the sewing machine in her strong arms. And soon Abner was standing on a low stool while Mrs. Delgado measured him. She unrolled the long tape measure, marked with inches. She put it around his waist and down his leg and across his shoulders. Already Abner could understand her better, because she mostly

said the same things. "Stand still." "Stand up straight." "Stop wiggling." But when she said that, it sounded more like "Stop weegling."

Abner's nose itched. He twisted his neck to see if he could rub it on his shoulder, and caught a flash of movement through the kitchen doorway. His brother and sisters had opened the jar of grasshoppers and spread them out on the table.

"Hold still, please," said Mrs. Delgado again. "What are you trying to see?"

Abner pointed through the doorway. "They're counting the grasshoppers they caught."

"Ah!" said Mrs. Delgado. "They have caught grasshoppers to eat!"

Abner looked at her. Was she serious?

"Not to eat," he said. "Just to get rid of them."

Mrs. Delgado almost dropped her tape measure. "Get rid of them? Oh, no! Such crunchy, delicious treats!"

Abner looked at her in horror. Tate, Derek, and Celia poked curious faces around the door.

Mrs. Delgado laughed. "Back in my home country, we would catch all the grasshoppers we could find. Then we would eat them like you eat pretzels!"

Abner didn't say what he was thinking. But his face showed it.

Mrs. Delgado laughed and laughed. Her upper arms shook, and she hugged herself to keep the laughter in. "You have never tried them, or you would not twist up your face like that, as if you had tasted something bad. I roast them with garlic and salt, and they are oh so good! My own little boy, he loves them. I make them for you for lunch, no?"

"No," said Abner firmly. "Wait—I mean yes, 'no' is the right word. I mean . . ." He looked at his brother and sisters, despairing.

Tate looked right back at him. "It would be a very *brave* thing," she said, "to eat a grasshopper."

A salty smell of garlic filled the house. It smelled like pretzels baking, only not quite. Abner stood perfectly still as Mrs. Delgado fitted the half-sewn pieces of his costume on him. He tried not to think about what was in the oven.

He heard a clatter and some scraping sounds from the kitchen. Derek was probably opening drawers. Celia was probably dropping silverware. And Tate was probably making the sandwiches.

Normally, Abner was fussy about his sand-wiches. If the sandwich was peanut butter and jelly, he liked his bread toasted. If it was ham and cheese, he liked Swiss cheese and extra ham. If it was tuna salad, he liked sweet pick-les chopped in with the celery.

But now he didn't care what they gave him, so long as it didn't include bugs. He looked at the picture of General Abner Willow. The man had been brave, sure, but had he ever eaten a *grasshopper?*

"There!" said Mrs. Delgado. "You can get down. And now to the kitchen!"

The four Willow children watched with horror as Mrs. Delgado removed a tray of small, lumpy brown objects from the oven. Even when they were baked, there was no hiding that they were bugs. Little legs stuck in the air like bent twigs. Big, crusty heads looked at them with glazed golden eyes.

Abner tried not to shudder.

Mrs. Delgado was humming to herself. She swept the grasshoppers off the tray and into a large bowl. She handed the bowl to Tate, who nearly dropped it.

"You will take them to the porch to cool, no?" said Mrs. Delgado. "Abner will help me carry my things out to the car. My neighbor, she cannot watch my little boy anymore today, so I will sew the rest at my home."

Abner felt a wave of relief as he stacked the bolts of fabric in Mrs. Delgado's backseat. She was leaving. Soon she would be gone, and she would never know if they ate the grasshoppers or not.

But as Mrs. Delgado walked out with her sewing machine, she stopped on the porch and set it down. "Now!" she said, beaming all over her dimpled face. "Let's see if you like these grasshoppers I have baked!"

Abner stared at the bowl of shiny brown bugs. He didn't think he could do it.

"Don't worry about the wings. They will not get stuck in your teeth," said Mrs. Delgado. "I pulled them off for you."

Derek clutched his stomach and turned away. Celia put her hands over her mouth.

Abner saw Mrs. Delgado's happy face begin

to look worried. Had they hurt her feelings? Maybe she missed the place where she had grown up, a place where everyone knew that grasshoppers were a perfectly good snack.

Just get it over with, he told himself. *You only have to eat one. You can barf later if you need to.*

Before he could change his mind, Abner popped a grasshopper in his mouth. It felt warm and twiggy, but he told himself it was just an extra-bumpy pretzel. He gritted his teeth and bit down. It crunched. And squished.

He swallowed very fast.

He ran his tongue around his teeth to make sure there were no legs stuck there. The taste that was left on his tongue was . . . sort of buggy. It wasn't nearly as bad as he had expected. He smiled at Mrs. Delgado in the joy of his relief.

"You like my grasshoppers?" she cried. "Wonderful, *bueno,* very good! And now who else will try?"

Celia and Derek put their hands behind their backs.

"I might," said Tate, "a little later."

Mrs. Delgado laughed again. She really was a remarkably cheerful person, Abner thought, for someone who liked to cook bugs.

"You will enjoy them," said Mrs. Delgado. "My little boy, he likes them very much, but I do not often have the time to catch them. And he is only two, so he cannot catch them very well on his own."

"Take some home for him!" urged Abner. "Take them all!"

Tate ran to the kitchen and returned with a plastic bag. "You can put them in this!"

"Oh, I couldn't take them all. I must leave enough for you, and your parents, too. But I will take a few," she said, scooping a handful into the bag. "I will save them for my little boy—all but this one." She popped it in her mouth, and the children heard the crunch.

"Mmmm! So good!" She hefted the sewing machine in her sturdy arms. "Your costume, it will be ready tomorrow morning. You come to my house at the corner of Oak and

Main Streets, no? The parade, it starts across the road, at the school." She walked to the car with a light, springy step. *"¡Adios!"* she called. "Goodbye!"

"Wow, she's really strong," said Tate. "She's almost bouncing on her toes, and she's carrying that heavy sewing machine."

"She's just a happy, bouncy sort of person," said Abner. He sat down, feeling good. He had done it. He had eaten a grasshopper, and none of the others had dared. Maybe he *was* getting braver, after all.

Derek and Celia were looking at him with awe. Tate gazed at the bowl, still half-filled with grasshoppers. "How was it, Abner?" she asked. "How did it taste?"

"Not bad," said Abner, "for a bug. But I don't want to eat any more. I almost barfed right then and there."

"No joke," said Derek. "It's *weird* to eat grasshoppers."

"I wonder," said Tate. "Maybe people just like the foods they're used to. I heard that people in other countries think the foods *we* eat are weird. Somebody told me once that only Americans like peanut butter."

"Really?" said Derek. "How could you not like peanut butter?"

Tate shrugged. "*I* don't know. I'm just telling you what I *heard*. Anyway, Mrs. Delgado and everybody in her country like grasshoppers. So they're probably worth a try."

Abner heard an unmistakable crunch. He looked up to see Tate with a grasshopper between her teeth.

Derek and Celia looked at Tate with disbelief.

"Hey, they're pretty good," said Tate, and she reached for another.

Abner's mouth fell open. Tate had wrecked everything. He only felt brave because he had done something no one else dared to do. So now that Tate had eaten a grasshopper, he would have to eat two. No, three—no, *four*—

Abner looked at Tate in horror. She had taken a whole handful! She was eating them like potato chips!

He pulled the bowl toward himself. "Listen," he said, "quit it, Tate! You wanted me to eat the grasshoppers, so I'm *eating* the grasshoppers! I'm going to eat all of them!"

He crammed the crunchy brown bugs into his mouth as if he were eating a whole bag of pretzels at one sitting. He blocked Tate with his shoulder as he scooped the bowl clean. He chewed and swallowed and did not throw up. And when he finished the last one, he leaned back and gave a long, satisfied belch.

There. Now he really *was* the bravest.

"Well, that was piggy," said Tate after a silence.

Derek grinned. "It was kind of awesome, though."

Celia gazed at her big brother with respect. "You ate a whole *bowl* of bugs."

"I sure did!" Abner was filled with sudden energy. "Come on, Seal," he said, calling her by her baby name. "I'll swing you around by your hands."

Celia stood up at once. That was one of her favorite things to do. She reached for Abner's hand and held on tight as he jumped off the porch.

He jumped off the porch, but he didn't stay on the ground. He bounced up. He bounced as high as the roof, and Celia bounced with him, her pigtails flying and her hand gripping Abner's in a panic.

Abner's brain went into shock. But his body reacted, even in the air. He grabbed Celia's free arm and pulled her in tight. He didn't know how he had jumped so high, but he knew he could not drop his little sister.

Tate and Derek stared, openmouthed. Their heads tilted backward, then forward, as Abner and Celia began to come down.

They hit the ground with a solid thud. Celia stumbled and clutched Abner with both hands. He took a quick step to get his balance, and they bounced up again.

Sproing! Up they went, higher than ever. Abner scraped his arm against a tree branch. Celia's hair got caught in some twigs and yanked painfully as she came down.

"Let go of me!" shrieked Celia as they dropped to the ground.

Abner let her hands go as he landed. He fell onto his knees and stared wildly at his brother and sisters.

"Don't move!" Tate called. "I'm coming!" She jumped off the porch steps and headed toward Abner and Celia. But she never got there.

Her first step bounced her high into the oak tree. She grabbed a branch, hung there, and looked down.

"Wow," said Derek. He leaped up. "It's magic! It's happening again!"

CHAPTER 3

Boing!

Derek jumped up and down and looked at his feet in disappointment. "Hey, it doesn't work for me."

"Me neither," said Celia, who was trying it herself.

Tate let go of her branch and climbed down. When her feet hit the ground, she sprang up again, and again. Finally she landed on her hands and knees next to Abner, breathing hard.

Carefully, she rolled over and sat on the grass, with her legs straight out in front of her.

"It must be grasshopper magic," she said. "That's why Derek and Celia can't jump like we can. They didn't eat any grasshoppers."

"But Mrs. Delgado didn't bounce like this," Abner argued.

"She only ate *one* grasshopper," said Tate.

"Plus, she's heavier," said Derek. "And she was carrying that big sewing machine."

"Sit on Abner's feet, Derek," Tate said. "Maybe you can keep him on the ground."

Derek sat on his brother's feet and gripped his legs. "Okay, now see if you can still jump."

Abner bent his knees a little. Then he tried a hop.

"Wheeeee!" cried Derek as they sailed into the air.

"Fall forward!" cried Tate as Abner and

Derek came down again. "Don't let your feet touch the ground!"

Abner did not want to fall forward. He thought he might squish Derek.

Thump!

"Let's keep bouncing!" shouted Derek as they went up again. "We're grasshoppers!"

Abner laughed out loud as the air whistled past his ears. If he had to be a grasshopper boy, he might as well enjoy it. He got a good grip under Derek's arms, and the next time they came down, Abner sprang up with all his strength. They bounced so high, they startled three crows right out of a tree. The boys leaped all over the yard in great, bounding grasshopper jumps, chasing the crows and whooping with glee.

Celia looked at Tate. "It *does* look like fun," she said. "I'm not scared anymore."

Tate bent over to let Celia get on her back. And then they were off, too, leaping, almost flying with each springy bound.

"Let's go on top of the house!" cried Derek.

Abner took three big jumps and dropped Derek gently on a part of the roof that was almost flat. Then he bounced once and landed on his hands and knees, his feet tucked up behind him. *"Yeeouch!"* He sat up on the roof shingles, rubbing his knees.

"It worked," said Derek. He stood up and shaded his eyes as Tate came in for a landing, with Celia on her back.

"Oooof!" said Tate, scraping to a stop. Celia tumbled off, and Tate caught her just before she slid out of reach.

"Careful," Abner told Celia. "If you and Derek fall off, you won't bounce."

The rooftop was patchy with moss, old

strips of tar paper, and shingles that looked as if they'd been there a long time. Abner and Tate didn't want to crawl over the rough shingles on their hands and knees. But Celia and Derek walked all over the roof, their bodies at a slant.

"Hey! There's my rubber ball!" Derek's voice came floating over the roof's peak. "It got stuck in the gutter!"

Celia had found the brick chimney top. She didn't want to mention it to the others, but she wasn't sure Santa could get down such a small hole.

Abner and Tate sat side by side, taking in the view. The house was at the top of a hill and was ringed with trees. Their long gravel driveway curved down to a stone arch bridge over a blue river, and after that were farmers' fields and barns and tall silos. The dust still hung over the gravel roads where Mrs. Delgado's car had passed. In the distance, they could see the clustered buildings of the town.

"I bet the parade will go down Main Street," said Tate. "Do you think you'll read your speech on the courthouse steps?"

Abner was hot and sweaty, and he didn't want to talk about the parade or the speech. He wiped his forehead and changed the subject. "Let's jump down and get some lemonade. I'm baking up here."

◕〜◕〜◉

The Willow children sat on the porch, cooling off. Abner and Tate had their feet up on the railing so they wouldn't accidentally start bouncing. Derek had found a book on insect facts and was reading parts of it out loud.

"Hey, listen," he said. "A grasshopper can leap twenty times the length of its body!"

"That sounds about right," said Abner, who had made some amazing leaps in the backyard.

"Let me see that," said Tate. She scanned the page and then said, "Here we go." She stabbed a sentence with her forefinger. " 'Grasshopper eggs are laid one to two inches underground, and stay there through the winter.' That's it! That's how the magic got in. The grasshoppers were underground all that time, just soaking it up."

"We'd better figure out how to deal with it, though, before Mom and Dad get home," said Abner.

Tate said, "Maybe we'll use it up faster if we keep on bouncing."

"Abner will have to bounce a lot more than Tate," said Celia. "She only ate a handful. He ate half a bowl."

Derek nodded. "He's got a lot more grass-hopper magic to get rid of. Hey, Abner, maybe we can weigh you down with rocks! We can make you as heavy as Mrs. Delgado, and you can carry heavy things, too, like Celia and me!"

"That might help," said Abner. "Only I ate so *many*. Mrs. Delgado just ate one."

"But she brought more home with her," Celia said. "When she eats them, she's going to *really* start bouncing."

"Mrs. Delgado isn't going to eat them," said Derek. "Remember? She said she was going to give them to—" He stopped abruptly.

There was a stricken silence. They all remembered what Mrs. Delgado had said.

"She's going to give them to her little boy," Tate finished in a whisper. "And he's only two."

The four Willows looked at one another. They knew the trouble a two-year-old could get into if he was able to bounce higher than his mother could reach.

"He could bounce into traffic," said Celia. "He might get run over!"

"He could bounce into a lake," said Derek. "He might drown!"

Tate's face was pale. "He could bounce high enough to hit a power line. He might get electrocuted." She turned to Abner. "We have to get those grasshoppers back!" She gave a great bounding leap toward the road.

"Wait!" Abner shouted, bouncing after her. "Stop!"

Tate looked at him wildly. "We *can't* wait. She might be giving him the grasshoppers right this minute!"

Abner shook his head. "First, let's call her house."

"Oh. Okay." Tate bounded back to the

porch, crashed into the banister to stop herself, and grabbed Derek's and Celia's hands. "Go in and look on the message board," she said. "Mom wrote down Mrs. Delgado's number there. I'll crawl inside and make the call."

Abner sat on the porch steps, thinking hard. The general wouldn't have ridden straight into battle without a plan. Abner wasn't going to, either. The first thing he had to figure out was how to keep the bouncing under control.

By the time Tate and the others came back, he had worked out a long, low bounce, a flatfoot shuffle, and a side-of-the-foot step. That would have to be enough. "Did you talk to Mrs. Delgado?" he asked.

Tate said, "No, but I left a message. I said not to let anyone eat the grasshoppers, because we had to show them to our dad to get the money."

"Not bad," Abner said. "It sounds kind of

selfish, but it's better than telling her they're magic. No grown-up would believe *that*."

"But we can't just wait and hope she'll bring them back," said Tate. "We have to *do* something."

"We will," said Abner. "We're going to bounce all the way to her house at Oak and Main."

"But people will see us!" said Tate.

Abner shook his head. "Not if we're careful. I've figured out how to bounce low. And we don't have to take the roads—we can bounce straight across the fields. That will get us there faster."

"Can I come, too?" asked Derek.

"And me?" added Celia.

Abner nodded. "We'll need both of you. Now listen. I have a plan."

The four Willows leaped over the fields, keeping their heads pointed forward, their bodies

almost flat. This was the long, low bounce. But bounding through the fields was like getting whipped with a million blades of grass. After a while it started to hurt.

They stopped after the third field to adjust the bungee cords that strapped Celia to Tate's back and Derek to Abner's.

"My face is getting scratched to death," said Tate. "Maybe we should take the road, Abner. When we see a car coming, we can duck into a ditch."

"Okay," said Abner. "Watch for dust in the air. On these gravel roads, you can see a car coming a long way off."

"You can taste a car a long time after it passes, too," said Tate, coughing. "Derek and Celia, keep your eyes and mouths closed while we're moving."

"We already are," said Celia, who had buried her face in Tate's shirt.

"Okay, everybody ready?" Abner looked around. "Let's go, troops."

The ditches were damp and weedy, and Abner and Tate had to drop to their knees in one whenever a car passed. By the time they got to the edge of town, their knees were grass-stained and muddy and their tennis shoes were sopping wet. But they were getting better at landing.

Derek shifted his weight on Abner's back. "That last car—I think somebody saw us. A little girl in the backseat waved."

"A little kid is okay." Abner brushed off his

knees. "Everybody will just tell her she has a good imagination."

"Yes," said Tate, "but we have to be more careful now."

Abner looked past a tall grove of trees. He saw a line of scrubby bushes, a vacant lot, and what looked like a gravel pit. Beyond that was the first building in town. It was very tall, with an odd shape like houses stacked up. A sign said it was the feed mill.

Abner glanced around. No one was watching. "Tate," he whispered, "let's jump up where we can see. Derek and Celia, hang on tight."

With a tremendous grasshopper bound, Abner leaped onto the middle roof of the feed mill. A second leap took him to the top. Tate thumped right behind him.

"I feel sick," said Derek, who had made the mistake of opening his eyes.

"Don't look down," Tate advised.

"*I'm* not going to," said Celia in a muffled voice. Her face was still pressed into Tate's back.

Abner didn't feel sick at all. He loved to climb trees, and he liked being up high, where he could see everything. But he was not up here just for fun. He had to figure out where Mrs. Delgado's house was.

The town spread out below him like a toy village. He could see the rectangles of streets and the square rooftops of houses. He could see the taller buildings in the center of town, all lined up on Main Street.

And right next to a central square, he could see a big building with a playground. That must be the school. He pointed it out to Tate.

She nodded. "Mrs. Delgado said her house was across the street from the school."

Abner squinted. There were three houses

across from the school. "It must be the black roof, the gray roof, or the red roof. I can't see her car, though."

"Maybe she's not back yet! Let's hurry!" said Derek.

"We can jump rooftop to rooftop," said Abner. "People don't usually look up."

"Okay," said Tate. "I just hope the grass-hopper magic doesn't wear off while we're jumping."

The breeze whipped past them as they soared downward. Abner put his arms out to the sides for balance, and Tate did the same. They landed with a quick, soft bump on the roof of the gro-cery store, bent their knees, and bounced up again at once. Below them, shoppers with carts loaded groceries into their cars. One little baby looked up, pointed with a fat finger, and cried, "Birdies!"

"*Big* birdies," muttered Derek.

"*Really* big," said Abner, waving at the baby.

"Look out!" called Tate. "Church steeple ahead!"

Abner dipped his right arm, raised his left, and leaned to one side. The steeple whooshed past and his foot scraped the white paint.

"You left a smudge," said Derek. Now that they were off the feed mill and bouncing, he was having fun again.

Abner didn't care that he had left a smudge. No one would see it, up that high. He was just glad that he hadn't crashed into the steeple. No more waving at babies, he told himself sternly. He had to watch where he was going.

But when they had bounced all the way to the red roof across from the school, Abner had a terrible sinking feeling in his stomach. Mrs. Delgado's green car was in the driveway.

"Maybe she's at the neighbor's, picking up her little boy," whispered Tate.

The four Willows dropped lightly to the grass in Mrs. Delgado's backyard. They undid the bungee cords, and Abner and Tate stuffed them in their pockets. Then Derek and Celia marched up the back steps to knock on the door.

Abner moved his toes the tiniest bit and bounced up a few feet to look in the kitchen window. On the first bounce, he saw a refrigerator, a stove, and Mrs. Delgado's back.

On the second bounce, he saw Mrs. Delgado moving away to answer the door.

And on the third bounce, he saw her little boy, strapped in a high chair and kicking happily.

Abner gripped the window frame and hung on. He pressed his nose to the glass.

In front of the two-year-old, on his tray, was a small pile of grasshoppers. As Abner watched, the little boy put one in his mouth and bit down.

CHAPTER 4

Hopper Trouble

"He's eating them!" Abner slid down beside Tate and told her what he had seen. "Keep your feet perfectly flat to shuffle forward," he said. "Go up the steps on the sides of your feet. We have to get inside and stop him from eating more."

The back door opened. "Why, it's the Willows! What are you doing here?" asked Mrs. Delgado.

Derek and Celia turned to look at Tate. She was the best at explaining things to grown-ups.

But Tate hadn't practiced the flat-foot shuffle as Abner had. When she took a step, she almost left the ground, and her toes were dragging.

"Celia!" Abner hissed. "Derek! Help her!"

Derek and Celia rushed to take her arms. They pulled down, and Tate shuffled forward slowly.

"Did you hurt your feet?" Mrs. Delgado came down the steps. "You are walking so—"

"Mrs. Delgado," Abner blurted out, "can we come in?"

"Of course. You must meet my Tomas!" Mrs. Delgado's broad back filled the doorway, and Tate whispered to the others quickly.

"Can I have a drink of water?" begged Derek as soon as he got in the kitchen, and Celia said, "Me too?"

Mrs. Delgado stood at the kitchen sink, filling two glasses. Abner stood in front of the high chair with Tate, blocking Mrs. Delgado's view of her son.

Tate tickled the little boy under the chin. Tomas looked up with big brown eyes.

Abner made a goofy face. He crossed his eyes and stretched his mouth wide with his fingers. The little boy laughed and reached out one pudgy fist. It was full of squashed grass-hoppers.

Abner glanced down at the tray. Tate was sweeping the rest of the grasshoppers into her pocket. "Keep him busy!" she whispered.

Abner stuck out his tongue and waggled it from side to side.

Tomas laughed again. Then he opened his hand and picked out one grasshopper. He put it carefully on Abner's tongue.

"How sweet!" cried Mrs. Delgado, bending over their heads. "Tomas wants to share!"

Abner stared at Tate with his mouth wide open. Grasshopper legs hung over his tongue.

"Better eat it," said Tate sternly.

"Or Tomas will," added Derek.

Abner shut his eyes. He crunched and swallowed.

"Tomas, have you eaten the rest already?" Mrs. Delgado looked down at the tray. "You should not eat so fast. You will get a tummy ache!"

Tomas didn't seem worried about a tummy ache. He was more interested in putting the rest of his grasshoppers into Abner's mouth.

"And now," said Mrs. Delgado, "you must tell me. How did you get here so fast? Did your mother drive you?"

Abner couldn't say anything. His mouth was full of grasshoppers that he didn't want to swallow.

"No," said Tate. "We . . . got a lift. From . . . Mr. Hopper."

Mrs. Delgado smiled. "People here, they are

so friendly. They give rides all the time. But why did you come?"

Abner, Derek, and Celia looked at Tate.

"We came to help you!" said Tate. "We came to babysit your little boy, so you could have more time to sew Abner's costume!"

⚬⚬⚬

The Willows didn't let Tomas's feet touch the ground. They carried him outside, where Abner spit out his mouthful of grasshoppers. Then they found Mrs. Delgado's old-fashioned stroller and strapped Tomas in. But he was a big boy, and his feet touched the footrest. The stroller bumped and jolted as if trying to bounce, and his body pressed up against the straps.

Tate bent over to check them. "The straps are holding him in," she said, "for now. But if they rip . . ."

Tomas laughed and banged his feet down. The straps creaked. The stroller jerked forward a few inches and tipped to one side.

Abner snatched at the handle and steadied the stroller. "Sit on the footrest, Celia!"

"I'm too big for a stroller," said Celia.

Tomas kicked again. "Too big!" he crowed. "*Tomas* too big!"

Tate caught his short legs in midair and glared at her sister. "Celia, sit *down*," she snapped.

"There's not enough room," Celia complained, but she wedged herself onto the footrest with her back to Tomas. When she put her feet on the ground, her knees were almost to her chin!

Tate set the little boy's legs on Celia's shoulders. "Hold his ankles," said Tate, "or he'll kick *you*."

Celia made a grumpy noise.

"Look, Seal, I'm getting on, too," said Derek. He stood at the back of the stroller, on the ledge meant for packages. "Now it's really weighed down."

"It's a good thing this stroller is built like a tank," said Abner.

Tate hung on to the handle along with Abner. With three children on it, the stroller was heavy enough to keep her on the ground. She gave a tiny push with her feet and the stroller leaped forward.

"Don't use your toes!" hissed Abner. He looked up to the window where Mrs. Delgado stood watching. He gave her a wide smile and an airy wave. He tried to keep his feet perfectly flat and not move his toes at all.

Mrs. Delgado opened the window. "Why don't you take Tomas over to the park?" she called. "He loves the bouncing horses!"

"Horsies!" cried Tomas. "Bouncy bouncy!"

They pushed the stroller slowly down the street. "He'll be bouncing enough without any horses to help him," muttered Abner.

"We've got to get him somewhere safe," said Tate, "where he can bounce it off."

But the children couldn't find a safe place to let Tomas bounce. Everywhere they went, there were people.

"Why is it so crowded?" asked Derek.

"Willow Days must have started already," said Tate. "Look." She pointed to a poster on a pole. "Tomorrow is the big parade. But today there's a horse show, a ball game, a pie-eating contest. . . ."

"Pie!" shouted Tomas, kicking his legs. "*Tomas* eat pie!"

"Ow!" said Celia.

"Pie! Pie! Pie! Pie!" Tomas banged the stroller with his chubby fists. "PIE!"

"Maybe we should feed him," Derek said. "That might keep him quiet until we find a bouncing place."

"Okay, okay." Abner dug in his pocket for the money he had brought, just in case. "There's a bakery on Main Street. We can get him a cookie."

"Cookie?" Tomas stopped kicking.

"I want one, too," said Celia, rubbing her shoulders. "*I'm* the one who got kicked."

"And I need to put some rocks in my pockets," Tate said. "My toes are cramping up from trying to walk this way."

Main Street was full of people. There were kids riding trikes with balloons tied to the handlebars. There were grown-ups eating hot dogs and waving to each other. And

there were some boys Abner's age carrying baseball bats.

Abner wished he were not pushing a baby stroller full of little kids. The boys were grinning as they looked at him.

Then the bakery door opened. Their mother came out with her arms full. "What on earth are you doing here?" she asked them.

CHAPTER 5

Runaway!

"Cookie!" shouted Tomas.

"We're babysitting Mrs. Delgado's little boy," said Tate in a hurry. "So she can sew Abner's costume."

Mrs. Willow's eyebrows went up. "I wish you had asked me first. Did Mrs. Delgado bring you to town?"

Tate didn't know what to say. She really didn't want to lie to her mother. But some things were just too hard to explain.

Tate was saved by the sound of a loud, high voice. It was Mrs. Gofish, calling to them.

"Oh, I'm so glad to see you!" Mrs. Gofish came bustling up. She was holding the strings of more balloons than Tate could count. "Maybe you children can help me."

Abner was worried. He did not want to help Mrs. Gofish anymore. It was bad enough that he had to be General Abner Willow in the parade. What did she want him to do now?

The others were wondering the same thing.

"What sort of help do you need?" asked Mrs. Willow.

"Cookie?" Tomas said hopefully. "Cookie? Cookie? Cookie?"

Mrs. Gofish laughed. "I'll buy cookies for all of you if you pass out these balloons," she said. "Give them to the children who don't have any yet. I have to help judge the horse show."

The children looked at one another.

Celia and Derek knew they had to stay on the stroller, to hold it down.

Tate and Abner knew they had to hang on to the stroller, to keep from bouncing up.

It would not be so easy to do all that and hand out balloons, too. And besides, wouldn't balloons give them even more lift?

But Mrs. Gofish was already tying the balloons to the stroller handle. Tate quietly picked up a few more rocks.

Mrs. Gofish bought a bag of cookies at the bakery window. Mrs. Willow tucked the bag into a side pocket of the stroller. "Don't eat them until you've handed out all the balloons," she said.

Abner didn't care about cookies. He wanted to get out of the crowd, fast. But he had to push the stroller slowly, or he would start to bounce.

Derek and Celia handed out balloons from the stroller. Tate tried to help, but even with rocks in her pocket, it was hard to keep from springing up with each careful step.

Abner looked straight ahead and didn't smile. He pushed the stroller past the grinning boys on the sidewalk and pretended he didn't see them.

"Hey, it's a kiddie parade!" one of them said.

Abner felt like leaving town and never coming back. This was worse than eating a bowl of grasshoppers. He kept on pushing the stroller right to the edge of town, where there was a grassy park, with a hill beyond.

"This is where they're going to have the horse show," Tate said. "See?" She pointed.

There were cars and trailers in front of the hill. Some people were leading their horses out of trailers. Others were setting up hay bales for hurdles. One rider was trying to get her horse to jump over a big bale of hay, but the horse kept backing away.

"We can't let Tomas bounce here," Tate said. "There are too many people already. And more are coming."

"I know," Abner said. "But the people will all be on this side of the hill. There won't be anybody on the other side."

And there wasn't, unless you counted a little white dog that sniffed at them. The Willows found a grassy spot behind some big rocks and a tree, perfect for bouncing.

"Let's have our cookies first," Tate said. "Tomas has been good and quiet this whole time. He should get an extra-big one."

"I'll pass them out," said Derek, reaching for the bag.

But there was no bag of cookies in the side pocket. And when they turned to look at Tomas, they could see why he had been so quiet. His cheeks were bulging. Cookie crumbs were falling from his mouth. And both his hands were inside the bakery bag.

"The little piggy!" Celia felt inside the bag. "There's nothing in here but crumbs! He ate them all!"

"Now he really will have a tummy ache," said Tate. She dumped the cookie crumbs on the ground. The little white dog trotted over to see if they were good to eat.

Abner undid the stroller straps and lifted Tomas out. "It's his own fault if he does," he said. "Anyway, let's hurry up and get him bouncing. Then the magic will start to wear off, I bet. Tate, you take first turn."

Tate tried. She took Tomas's hand and gave

a little spring. But she only got six inches off the ground, and Tomas bounced higher than her head.

"Ow! He'll pull my arm off!" Tate cried.

"Hang on to him!" Abner said. "Your grasshopper magic is all used up!"

Tate pulled a giggling Tomas down and held him tightly. "I *thought* it was getting easier to walk without bouncing," she said. "You'll have to bounce with him now, Abner."

Tomas wiggled in her arms. "Tomas *bounce*!"

"Yeah, okay." Abner took hold of his hands. "Let's go, buddy. Bounce! Bounce! Bounce! Boun— Oh, *no*!"

Everyone ducked out of the way as Tomas threw up, right in the air. Bits of cookie and chunks of grasshopper came flying down, wet and smelling of vomit.

"Eeew," said Derek. He looked at the chunks on the ground and made a face.

"Don't *land* in it!" called Tate.

Abner stretched his legs to miss the worst of the mess. He tried to set Tomas down on a clear space, but the little boy landed right on a chunk and slipped.

Tomas sat down suddenly on his bottom, looking surprised. Then he started to cry.

"That's what happens when you eat a whole bag of cookies," said Celia. She didn't feel one bit sorry for Tomas. He had eaten her cookie, and now he had wasted it.

"Babies don't know any better." Tate dug in her pocket for a tissue, but couldn't find anything but the grasshoppers she had taken from Tomas's tray. She flung them onto the ground.

Derek reached into the stroller's pocket and found the napkins from the bakery. "Here, use these."

Tate wiped Tomas's face. "Hold still," she told him. "You don't want to be sick again."

Tomas wiggled and kicked, but Tate held him firmly until his face was clean. Then she looked up to see Abner staring at them both.

"What?" said Tate.

Abner grinned. It had been a very hard day, but things were looking up. "Tomas spit up all the grasshoppers," he said. "Look at him! He's kicking the ground and he's not bouncing!"

"Well, it's about time something went right," said Tate. "Now the only one who has to get rid of grasshopper magic is you."

"It will take Abner a lot longer," said Celia. "Because he ate more grasshoppers than you or Tomas."

"A *lot* more," said Derek. He looked at Abner. "Do you want me to punch you in the stomach? You might barf your grasshoppers, too."

"No thanks," Abner said. "Nice offer, though. Really."

"Just trying to help," Derek said.

Abner ignored this. "At least we can take Tomas back to his mother now. Put him in the stroller, Tate, and let's roll."

But Tomas didn't want to go into the stroller. "No!" he said.

"Oh, come *on*, Tomas," Tate said. She tried to push his feet through the stroller's leg holes, but Tomas stiffened his fat little knees and stuck out his lower lip.

"NO!" he said again. "Tomas *down*!"

"Okay, fine." Tate put the little boy down on the grass. "But you have to hold someone's hand."

"NO!" said Tomas.

Derek grinned at him. "I bet I know your favorite word."

Tomas ran away, giggling. Derek and Celia ran after him, and each grabbed a hand.

"Keep going," Tate called. "We'll catch up."

Abner said, "Better hop in the stroller, Tate. I need some kind of weight to hold me down if I'm going to walk."

Tate sat in the stroller with her legs hanging over the front and her arms dangling to the ground. "I look like a fool."

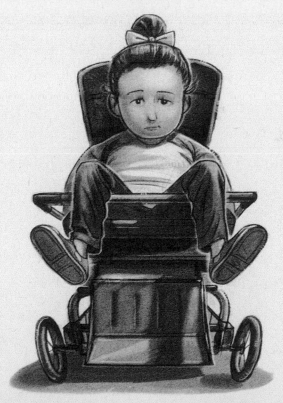

"Join the club," said Abner, who hadn't forgotten the grinning boys.

He pushed forward with his feet, and the stroller bumped over the rough ground. He passed the little white dog, who was sniffing at the grasshoppers Tate had thrown on the grass. When he rounded the curve of the hill, he saw that the horse show had begun.

Derek and Celia had sat down on the side of the hill, with Tomas between them. They had a good view of the hurdles and the track for the horses.

The crowd clapped as a black horse and its rider went over three hay bales, one right after the other. The next in line was a pale horse with a dark mane and tail.

"Horsie!" shouted Tomas, and he jumped up. Derek and Celia pulled him down.

"Keep hold of him," called Abner.

Derek and Celia turned their heads to answer. Then they started to laugh. They pointed their fingers.

"What?" Abner turned around. Behind him, on the other side of the hill, a little white dog—a surprised-looking dog—was bouncing high.

"Oh, no," moaned Abner.

"Oh, *NO!*" shouted Tate. But she wasn't looking at the dog. "Tomas, *stop!*"

In a half second, Abner saw it all. Derek and Celia had let go of Tomas to point at the bouncing dog. Tomas had taken off, straight for the track. And the pale horse was already jumping the hurdles, going fast.

Tomas was behind one of the hay bales, right in the path of the horse. The rider didn't seem to see him.

Other people had seen. Faces in the crowd

were filled with horror. Mouths were open, shouting. As if in slow motion, Abner saw people move forward to save the little boy. But in that half second, when everything seemed to freeze, Abner knew they would be too late.

Before he knew he had made a decision, Abner's knees bent and his feet flexed. He sprang out and down, in a long, low grasshopper bounce. The sound of thundering hooves filled his ears as he grabbed Tomas around his middle and pulled him in close, as if he were a football.

Abner twisted in midair. He hit the ground with a thud, ramming his shoulder, banging his head, scraping his ear. Then everything went dark.

CHAPTER 6

Town Hero

Abner opened his eyes. He was flat on his back. Above him was the sky, and a crowd of faces. Everyone was making a lot of noise.

"Mom?" Abner said.

"Oh, Abner, you're all right!" said his mother. She wiped her eyes.

Abner struggled to sit up. "Is Tomas okay?" He looked around.

"Tomas is fine," said Mrs. Willow. "You

saved him, sweetheart. His mother already came and took him home. Now lie down again. Your head is bleeding."

Abner felt something drip down the side of his forehead. Suddenly he felt woozy. He lay back and closed his eyes. Over him, the voices kept on talking.

"He's a hero!"

"What a leap! I've never seen anything like it."

"Well, the body can do amazing things in times of stress."

"I'd like to see him try out for the track team. With a long jump like that, we'd be sure to win State!"

Another voice came closer. Strong, expert hands turned his head this way and that. A bandage was wrapped around his head. "Do you think you can walk, son?" asked the town doctor.

Abner wiggled his toes and felt a certain bounce. "Maybe," he said. He looked around for his brother and sisters. "I need someone to lean on, though."

Tate came up at once and took one arm. Derek and Celia took the other.

"But don't you want a grown-up to help

you?" asked their mother. "Someone stronger, in case you fall?"

"No thanks," Abner said.

Tate spoke up firmly. "He needs us."

Derek whispered to Celia, "Yeah, he needs us to *hold him down!*"

Abner did the flat-foot shuffle over to his mother's car. Once he was home, he put his feet up. He even napped in a chair in the sun.

It was a good thing he did. Because late that night, when everyone else was asleep, Abner went outside to bounce in the moonlight. He bounced half the night, until the grasshopper magic was all used up. And then he went to bed.

᭟᭟᭟

The next morning, Abner waited at the stable for his horse to be saddled for the parade. He was wearing the uniform that Mrs. Delgado had sewn, and he had a real sword from the historical society, too. Mrs. Gofish had said that since Abner was a real hero, he shouldn't have to carry a fake sword.

Even better, Abner had a bloody bandage around his head. His mother had wanted to give him a clean one for the parade, but he wouldn't let her. The dried blood was perfect for a war hero.

"Pssst! Hey, Abner!"

Abner looked. Peeking at him from the doorway of the stable were his brother and sisters.

"We wanted to say good luck," said Tate. She came forward and patted the big brown horse on the nose. "Do you have your speech?"

Abner touched the vest pocket of his uniform, and the folded paper inside made a crinkling sound. "It's right here." He had practiced it that morning, and it wasn't too bad. It was short, at least.

"Is your head better?" asked Celia. She gazed at him with worried eyes. It was the third time she had asked.

Derek said, "I guess you don't need bravery practice anymore," and everyone laughed. "Can I see your sword?" he asked.

Abner showed him the sword. Then the horse was ready, and the others had to back away as it was led out of the stable. Abner put his left foot in the stirrup, bounced up, and swung his right leg over the horse's back. It was hard, but he did it the first time. There was a little extra spring in his feet that he hadn't had two days ago.

Did a little of the grasshopper magic stay for good? Maybe he would go out for track, after all.

The others left to find a good parade-watching spot. "Salute us when you pass, okay?" Derek called, and then they were gone.

The stableman showed Abner how to hold the reins, and then walked alongside, just in case. The horse moved under Abner, its hooves making a *clip clop clop* sound on the pavement. Its broad back was covered with hair so short and groomed that it shone in the sun. A warm smell of horse filled Abner's nose.

His parents had told him that he didn't have to ride in the parade if he didn't feel well enough. And he had thought about staying home. But Mrs. Delgado had worked hard on his uniform. Besides, Abner had already pushed a baby stroller full of kids and balloons down Main Street, in his own personal kiddie parade. After that, riding a horse in a real parade didn't seem hard at all. He still felt a little twinge when he thought about reading the speech, but he shrugged it off. He guessed he would be as brave as he needed to be.

And it was fun to hear all the comments as he passed.

"Yes, sir, I'm telling the truth!" said a large man with a red face. "I swear, that dog was bouncing! I don't mean jumping, I mean bouncing higher than your head!"

Abner chuckled as they turned onto Main Street. The man was going to have a hard time getting anyone to believe *that* story.

"Abber! Abber!" someone shouted, and Abner looked down to see Mrs. Delgado and Tomas. The little boy was waving as hard as he could wave. "Horsie! Horsie, Abber!"

Abner waved back. "Hey, Tomas!"

Mrs. Delgado called, "My hero!"

Abner swayed gently with each stride of the horse. The sky was blue, somewhere a band started to play, and all at once Abner was happy. He might not be as brave as General Abner Willow, but he was brave enough. And even though grasshopper magic, just like every other kind of magic on Hollowstone Hill, had led to trouble, still it had been amazing. He looked up at the roof-tops and wished for a moment that he could bound over them again.

But riding a horse was exciting, too. He saw his parents in the crowd, and he waved. Beside them were Tate and Derek and Celia, and right next to them were the boys from yesterday— the ones who had laughed as he pushed the stroller down the street.

They weren't laughing now. They were eye-ing his bloody bandage with respect.

Abner gave the salute he had practiced that morning in the mirror. And his brother and sisters, and the grinning boys from yesterday, saluted right back.

The End

About the Author

Lynne Jonell is the author of the popular *Emmy and the Incredible Shrinking Rat,* a *Booklist* Editors' Choice and one of *School Library Journal*'s Best Books of the Year, as well as the first two books about the Willow family, *Hamster Magic* and *Lawn Mower Magic*. She has also written three other novels and seven picture books. Lynne has never eaten a grasshopper, but that's only because she hasn't found a magic one.